For Lalla
lots of love, Mum
V.F.

For Amelia
B.F.

Text copyright © 1995 by Vivian French
Illustrations copyright © 1995 by Barbara Firth

All rights reserved.

First U.S. edition 1995

Library of Congress Catalog Card Number 95-68294

ISBN 1-56402-614-0

2 4 6 8 10 9 7 5 3 1

Printed in Hong Kong

The pictures in this book were done in pencil and watercolor.

Candlewick Press
2067 Massachusetts Avenue
Cambridge, Massachusetts 02140

A Song for Little Toad

by
Vivian French

illustrated by
Barbara Firth

CANDLEWICK PRESS
CAMBRIDGE, MASSACHUSETTS

Old Mother Toad
was singing to her baby:

"Croak croak croak,
Sleep, my little sweet one.
Croak croak croak,
Close your eyes and sleep."

But Little Toad didn't
want to sleep. His eyes
were bright and shining,
and he stared all around.

A sheep was standing chewing in the field. He heard Old Mother Toad singing, and he saw Little Toad's bright eyes.

"Old Mother Toad," he baaed, "Little Toad will never sleep if you make that horrid croaking noise. You must sing him a soft and soothing song like this:

Baaaaa . . . Baaaaa . . . Baaaaa . . . "

"Oh dear," said Old Mother
Toad, "how foolish I am."
She began to rock Little
Toad to sleep.
"*Baaaaa . . . Baaaaa . . .*
Baaaaa . . ." she sang.
Little Toad's eyes opened
wide in surprise.

A duck was swimming
up the river with her
little ones behind her.
She heard Old Mother
Toad singing, and she
saw Little Toad's
shining eyes.

"Old Mother Toad," she quacked,
"Little Toad will never sleep
if you make that silly baaing
noise. You must sing him
a cheerful song
like this:

Quack!
Quack!

Quackitty
quack!"

"Oh dear," said
Old Mother Toad,
"how foolish I am."

She rocked Little
Toad to and fro.

Quack!

"Quack!

quack!"

Quackitty

Little Toad sat up in
his cradle and stared
at his mother.

A nightingale was perched in
a tree. He heard Old Mother
Toad singing, and he saw Little
Toad's wide open eyes.
"Old Mother Toad," he sang,
"Little Toad will never sleep if you
make that dreadful quacking noise.
You must sing him a sweet and
gentle lullaby."
And the nightingale
began to sing.

He sang of the quiet velvet night,
and he sang of the glimmering
evening star. He sang of the rustle
of the tall dark reeds, and he sang
the song of the rippling river.

The sheep and the duck and
Old Mother Toad listened,
and there was a silver tear
in Mother Toad's eye.

"That was a truly
wonderful song," she
said as the nightingale
bowed and flew away.
She sighed a long, sad sigh.
"I can never sing a song
as wonderful as that."
And the silver tear fell
on Little Toad's cradle.

"Mother! Mother!"
Little Toad called.
Mother Toad looked
at Little Toad lying
wide awake, his eyes
bright and shining.
"Little Toad," she
said, "when will
you ever sleep?"

Little Toad looked at his mother.
"Sing me my own song," he said.
"You have the most beautiful voice
in all the whole wide world.
Sing me my own song."

So Old Mother Toad sang:

"Croak croak croak,
Sleep, my little sweet one.
Croak croak croak,
Close your eyes and sleep."

And Little Toad closed
his eyes and slept.